by **Sarah Hines Stephens**

# BACKWARDS
# BOW-WOW

*illustrated by*
**Art Baltazar**

**Superman created by
Jerry Siegel and Joe Shuster**
by special arrangement with the Jerry Siegel family

raintree
a Capstone company — publishers for children

# Starring...

## KRYPTO
### THE SUPER-DOG

## BIZARRO KRYPTO

## ACE
### THE BAT-HOUND

## STREAKY
### THE SUPER-CAT

## ALFRED PENNYWORTH
### BATMAN'S BUTLER

# CONTENTS

## SUPER-PET HERO FILE 001:
# KRYPTO

heat & X-ray vision

super-hearing

super-smell

flight

freeze breath

super-speed

S-shield

**Super hero owner:**
**SUPERMAN**

**Species:** Super-Dog
**Place of birth:** Krypton
**Weakness:** Kryptonite
**Favourite food:** Ka-pow Chow

**Bio:** The childhood pet of the Man of Steel, Krypto the Super-Dog has the same powers as his heroic master.

## SUPER-PET ENEMY FILE 001:
# BIZARRO KRYPTO

ice & X-ray vision

super-hearing

flight

super-smell

flame breath

backwards S-shield

super-speed

**Super-villain Owner:**
## BIZARRO

**Bio:** When Krypto the Super-Dog crashed on Htrae, the Bizarros created his evil twin, Bizarro Krypto.

**Species:** Bizarro Dog
**Place of birth:** Htrae
**Weakness:** Blue kryptonite
**Favourite food:** Pineapple upside-down cake

# Chapter 1

# BACKWARDS PLANET

# SMAAAASH!

Shortly after midnight, an alien shuttle crashed down in the city of Metropolis. The strange rocket ship scraped across a car park. A trail of sparks streamed out behind it.

**SKREEECH!** The shuttle skidded to a halt next to a skip. A door in the side of the craft opened, and out stepped a white dog. The alien canine had a large head and red eyes. He was strong and wore a flowing red cape.

The alien looked a lot like Krypto

the Super-Dog, but he was actually

the exact opposite.

He was **Bizarro Krypto!** He had

never meant to land on Earth.

Bizarro Krypto was the only passenger on board a shuttle from the planet **Htrae**. The shuttle had flown far off course. It had become caught in Earth's gravity.

From the spaceship's window, Bizarro Krypto had watched the round planet growing closer and closer. It looked very, very different from his home planet.

**"Good bumpy landing,"** said Bizarro

Krypto. The alien canine climbed out

of the shuttle.

He shook himself off. Then he

walked out into the middle of the

car park.

The moon was full. The car park

was empty, and the shops were closed.

Bizarro Krypto started to worry. On

Htrae, the shops were always busy at

night. Where was everyone?

Bizarro Krypto walked through Metropolis. He passed more closed shops. He passed dark houses full of sleeping people.

Bizarro Krypto did not understand why people would sleep at night!

Moments later, the Sun started to rise. People began to wake up. Bizarro Krypto was stunned by what he saw in the light. Peeking through house windows, he saw dogs lying and eating on the floor. Humans sat on sofas and at tables.

That was not all! The more Bizarro

Krypto looked, the more confused and

worried he became. The people and

animals on this round planet were all

backwards. **Nothing made any sense!**

Bizarro Krypto was about to go back to his ship. Suddenly, a man in a dressing gown opened his front door. A small puppy scampered out.

Bizarro Krypto stopped to watch what would happen next. The young dog picked up a newspaper and trotted back to drop it at the man's feet.

"RUFF! RUFF! RUFF!"

"Good dog!" said the man.

Then he reached down and patted his dog. He handed her a chew bone.

Bizarro Krypto thought it was weird for a dog to fetch a newspaper for a person. On Htrae, people gave papers to dogs so they could chew them and make reading the news harder.

Still, that was not the strangest thing Bizarro Krypto saw. As he watched, the small dog took the bone. She ran off and dug a hole in the garden. **PLOP!** Then she dropped the bone into it!

Bizarro Krypto could not take it. **"Stop,"** he barked. **"You no do that!"**

The chew bone belonged in a frame. It was nasty and ugly and needed to be on display so all could enjoy it!

The little dog looked up, confused. "I'm saving it for later," she said shyly.

**"No, no, no!"** Bizarro Krypto said. He did not have time to explain what the dog was doing wrong. She ran off barking towards the fence.

Bizarro Krypto could not believe his eyes. The dog was chasing a cat!

Bizarro Krypto was more baffled than ever. What was a dog doing chasing a cat? It was like nothing he had ever seen.

Feeling a little shaken, Bizarro Krypto walked to the city centre. **The creatures of Earth needed his help.**

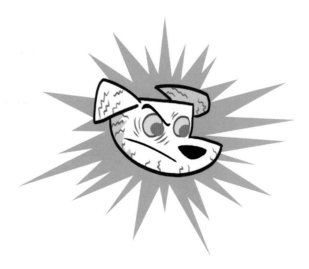

# Chapter 2

# A SHOCKING DISPLAY

The people and animals of Earth were starting their day. Bizarro Krypto thought they were doing it all wrong.

He had never seen dogs wearing collars. Collars were for humans! He had never seen people walk dogs on leashes. Those were for humans, too!

Then Bizarro Krypto saw the most shocking thing of all. Through the windows of the Museum of Natural History, the alien dog spotted an enormous skeleton. It was a dinosaur skeleton, clean and shiny.

**"That not good,"** Bizarro Krypto growled. **"That not good at all."**

On Htrae, big dry bones like those had to be buried. Only meaty, stinky bones were hung up for display. Huge bones like those in the museum, without anything to chew on, were too terrifying to show to the public.

Below the enormous skeleton, people stood still and stared. Bizarro Krypto thought they were frozen in horror. He had to help them. Nobody should have to look at such awful bones!

With incredible speed, Bizarro

Krypto burst into the museum.

**WOOOOSH!**

He grasped one of the giant bones

in his jaws and flew towards the door.

Alarms sounded. People screamed.

"They happy," he said. "I helping."

Outside, Bizarro Krypto spotted

a large grassy area. It was a park.

**THUD!** He touched down and started

digging. Dirt flew out of the hole faster

than wind from a hurricane. **FWOOOM!**

When the hole was finished, Bizarro Krypto flew back and forth carrying bones. He had dug a pit so huge a house could have fitted inside! Soon, he would have all the bones hidden in it. The people of Earth would be safe.

Bizarro Krypto was proud. He did not hear the sirens coming.

WEE-OOO! WEE-OOO!

"Stop! Police!" one of the officers shouted. Six police had formed a line to block Bizarro Krypto from going back into the museum.

Bizarro Krypto did not stop. He flew right past the police. **WHOOSH!** They tried to catch him in a net, but it was useless against the dog's alien powers.

**"We need help!"** one of the police officers shouted.

The officer was right. The only Earth creatures with enough power to stop a Bizarro dog were a pack of Super-Pets.

One of the officers put out the call, and just in time. Inside the museum, Bizarro Krypto had begun to pull apart the skeleton of a whale.

Moments later, the real **Krypto the Super-Dog** and **Ace the Bat-Hound** arrived at the scene.

"Let's go!" Krypto barked. "That crazy dog is destroying the museum!"

"Wait," Ace cautioned. "He looks a little like you."

Krypto shook his head. "No, he doesn't," he said gruffly. **"He's a bad guy. Bad guys don't look like me."**

Ace did not move. He was a good detective. He wanted to wait a moment to work out what was happening.

Through his mask, Ace watched Bizarro Krypto flying back and forth, carrying and burying bones. He definitely did look like Krypto, but he did not act like him.

The people at the museum had started throwing rubbish at the strange dog, trying to make him stop. Their attention only made him tear down the displays faster.

**"You no have to say thank you,"**

Bizarro Krypto told the crowd. He

ducked his head shyly. The people did

not understand him.

Bizarro Krypto thought they were

being nice. On Htrae, throwing rubbish

was a way to show how much you

liked something.

Ace did not know this. **All he knew**

**was that something was very**

**wrong.**

**"Come on! Let's stop this pooch,"**

Krypto said.

"We can give it a try," Ace agreed.

"But there's more going on here than

meets the eye."

Krypto had no idea what his friend

was talking about. The Super-Dog

stepped out to block the Bizarro's path.

Krypto let out a blast of icy breath to

stop this backwards dog in his tracks.

Bizarro Krypto dropped his bone.

Then he fired a warm blast of his own.

The two streams of air met, creating a

swirling vortex. **It was a stand-off!**

While Krypto and his reverse twin were busy, Ace moved. He grabbed the stolen bone and dragged it back to the museum. The crowd that had gathered gave him a loud cheer.

Bizarro Krypto caught on. He sent one last blast of hot breath at Krypto and turned to face the Bat-Hound.

**FWOOOOOSH!**

**"Bad dog,"** Bizarro Krypto barked at the Super-Pet. **"You frighten poor people. Bad."**

The backwards bow-wow snatched

the bone back easily. Then he flew over

to the giant hole he had dug.

"I helping," said Bizarro Krypto.

**"Helping?"** Ace repeated the word

to himself. **"Bad dog."**

Then Ace remembered something. Batman had told him about **Bizarro World** once. His crime-fighting partner had explained that the **Bizarros** were different from Earthlings. Their world was the exact opposite of Earth.

The trouble was, their ways made no sense here. Batman had also explained to Ace that because the Bizarros were just as strong and powerful as Earth's super heroes, they were extremely hard to control. Their ideas could be harmful even if they meant well.

If this other Krypto was a Bizarro from Htrae, the best thing the Super-Pets could do would be to send him home. **But how?**

# Chapter 3

# NONSENSE

**"Krypto!"** Ace called to his friend. "Keep an eye on Bizarro. I'll be back."

Without stopping to explain, Ace took off. He had to find whatever had brought Bizarro Krypto to Earth. They were going to need it to send the backwards bow-wow home again.

Krypto watched Ace running down the street. He was not sure what the other dog was doing, but he knew Ace liked to have a plan. He also knew that Ace's plans were usually good.

All Krypto needed to worry about was his odd opposite. Drawing a deep breath, he turned and tried again to freeze Bizarro Krypto in his tracks. Bizarro Krypto fought back with fiery breath. **FWOOOOOM!**

*Oh well,* Krypto thought. *If I can't stop him, at least I can keep him busy.*

Krypto was drawing a big breath when he picked up a new sound with his sensitive ears. It was the soothing purr of a cat.

"**Streaky!**" shouted the Super-Dog.

Krypto was relieved that another Super-Pet was coming to join him, but he was not sure Streaky would be much help.

**Supergirl's orange cat** did not leave his home often. He liked to take naps during the day and fight crime at night. Still, it was a good thing he had answered the call.

The Super-Dog was just about to deliver one more chilly gust when he saw Bizarro Krypto **freeze in his tracks.**

# WHUMP!

Streaky landed beside the Super-Dog. **"What's the problem?"** he asked, casually licking his paw.

Krypto did not answer. He was staring at Bizarro Krypto.

The alien dog still had not moved. His eyes were wide. He tried to blow out another hot breath, but coughed and staggered backwards instead.

He was afraid of something, and that something had to be Streaky!

Krypto had seen dogs that were afraid of Streaky before, but usually not until the cat revealed his powers. Bizarro Krypto was freaked out before Streaky had done a thing.

**"He's afraid of cats!"** Krypto said

aloud, trying not to laugh.

**"Then this should be fun,"** Streaky

purred. **"Where do we want him?"**

"Away from the museum," Krypto

answered.

Streaky flew right at Bizarro Krypto.

The frightened dog set off at top speed.

He fled up towards the clouds. The

real Krypto and Streaky flew after him.

They had him on the run!

"This is purrfect," Streaky shouted to Krypto. He flexed his claws. "But what should we do now?"

Krypto sniffed the air. Ace was near by. He pricked up his ears – Ace was calling to them.

"Chase him this way," Krypto said.

Streaky picked up the pace and chased Bizarro Krypto in the new direction. In moments, they were in the car park where Bizarro Krypto had crash-landed.

Ace was there with Alfred, Batman's butler. Alfred had a way with gadgets. He was tinkering with Bizarro Krypto's spaceship.

**"There you are, sir,"** Alfred said to Ace. He gave the silver craft a pat. **"All ready to go."**

Ace barked up to the Super-Pets flying overhead. Streaky and Krypto knew just what to do. Bizarro Krypto knew what to do, too! He flew to his ship and scrambled aboard.

Using his nose, Bizarro Krypto pushed the button that sealed the hatch. He prepared for take-off.

**"Nothing make sense here,"** the odd dog muttered to himself as he took off. Earthlings were beyond help.

Watching from the ground, the Super-Pets were happy to see Bizarro Krypto go. He may have meant well, but he would be better off on his own square planet, where everything made complete nonsense.

END

# KNOW YOUR HERO PETS

1. Krypto
2. Streaky
3. Beppo
4. Comet
5. Ace
6. Robin Robin
7. Jumpa
8. Whatzit
9. Storm
10. Topo
11. Ark
12. Hoppy
13. Batcow
14. Big Ted
15. Proty
16. Gleek
17. Paw Pooch
18. Bull Dog
19. Chameleon Collie
20. Hot Dog
21. Tail Terrier
22. Tusky Husky
23. Mammoth Mutt
24. Dawg
25. B'dg
26. Stripezoid
27. Zallion
28. Ribitz
29. Bzzd
30. Gratch
31. Buzzoo
32. Fossfur
33. Zhoomp
34. Eeny

1

2

3

4

5

6

7

8

9

10

11

12

13

14

15

16

17

18

19

20

21

22

23

24

25

26

27

28

29

30

31

32

33

34

# KNOW YOUR VILLAIN PETS

1. Bizarro Krypto
2. Ignatius
3. Rozz
4. Mechanikat
5. Crackers
6. Giggles
7. Joker Fish
8. Chauncey
9. Artie Puffin
10. Griff
11. Waddles
12. Dogwood
13. Mr. Mind
14. Sobek
15. Misty
16. Sneezers
17. General Manx
18. Nizz
19. Fer-El
20. Titano
21. Bit-Bit
22. X-43
23. Dex-Starr
24. Glomulus
25. Whoosh
26. Pronto
27. Snorrt
28. Rolf
29. Tootz
30. Eezix
31. Donald
32. Waxxee
33. Fimble
34. Webbik

 1
 2
 3
 4

 5
 6
 7
 8

 9
 10
 11
 12

 13
 14
 15
 16

 17
 18
 19
 20

 21
 22
 23
 24

 25
 26
 27
 28

 29
 30
 31
 32
 33
 34

# JOKES

What do you call a dog in a desert?

What?

A hot dog!

What kind of dog likes to take baths?

Not sure.

A shampoodle!

What do dogs like to eat for breakfast?

I give up.

Pooched eggs!

# GLOSSARY

**attention** notice taken of something

**Earthling** being from planet Earth

**gravity** force that pulls things down towards the surface of Earth

**hurricane** storm with high winds that starts in the ocean

**museum** place where interesting historical, scientific, or artistic objects are displayed

**sensitive** able to react to the slightest change

**vortex** swirling whirlpool of water or air

# MEET THE AUTHOR

## Sarah Hines Stephens

Sarah Hines Stephens has written more than 60 books for children about all kinds of characters, from Jedi to princesses. When she is not writing, gardening, or saving the world by teaching people about recycling, Sarah enjoys spending time with her heroic husband, two kids, and super friends.

# MEET THE ILLUSTRATOR

## Eisner Award-winner Art Baltazar

Art Baltazar defines cartoons and comics not only as a style of art, but as a way of life. Art is the creative force behind *The New York Times* best-selling, Eisner Award-winning, DC Comics series Tiny Titans, and the co-writer for *Billy Batson and the Magic of SHAZAM!* Art draws comics and never has to leave the house. He lives with his lovely wife, Rose, big boy Sonny, little boy Gordon, and little girl Audrey.

# ART BALTAZAR says:

## Read all the DC SUPER-PETS stories today!

Raintree is an imprint of Capstone Global Library Limited, a company
incorporated in England and Wales having its registered office at 264 Banbury
Road, Oxford, OX2 7DY – Registered company number: 6695582

www.raintree.co.uk
myorders@raintree.co.uk

First published by Picture Window Books in 2012
First published in the United Kingdom in 2012
The moral rights of the proprietor have been asserted.

Art Director and Designer: Bob Lentz
Editors: Donald Lemke and Vaarunika Dharmapala
Creative Director: Heather Kindseth
Editorial Director: Michael Dahl

ISBN 978 1 4747 6446 9 (paperback)
21 20 19 18 17
10 9 8 7 6 5 4 3 2 1

**British Library Cataloguing in Publication Data**
A full catalogue record for this book is available from the British Library.

Printed and bound in India